Isabella

and Her
Polka Dot Umbrella

by Carla Forrest

Illustrated by Qoinne Larsen

New Year Publishing, LLC

144 Diablo Ranch Court, Danville, CA 94506 USA

To my Isabella, who I love more than
words can say ...
And to Elvis, we miss you so much and
hope you are chasing squirrels in Heaven
— C.F.

To my family
— Q.L.

This is the true story of a girl named Isabella,
Her big brown dog named Elvis,
and her polka dot umbrella.

Now Isabella is a busy sort of girl,
never can sit still.
When she makes poor Elvis exercise,
he always gets his fill.

Her daddy bought her a big
trampoline to try and wear her out.
She jumps and jumps and jumps all day,
but at night she still runs about.

Her mommy took her to gymnastics
class, to see if she would tire.
After stretching, rolling, and tumbling
for hours, she was even more haywire.

One Saturday Isabella awoke
to a rainy, gloomy day.
Her mommy took one look outside and said,
"Oh no, this is not okay!"

Her mommy got out her raincoat and galoshes
and said, "Here, wear this Isabella.
Oh, and don't forget one more thing:
your polka dot umbrella."

Mommy sent Isabella and Elvis out into the rainy day. They took one look around the gloom and they began to play.

They jumped from puddle to puddle,
caught raindrops on their tongue.
They hid beneath the trampoline
and lots of songs were sung.

Then something happened, much
to Isabella's surprise;
Things began to change
right before her very eyes.

Isabella's umbrella became a circus tent,
and Elvis her sidekick clown.
They walked across a tightrope,
and began to dance around.

The umbrella turned into a hot air balloon, and floated way up high. Isabella and Elvis jumped inside and rode it through the sky.

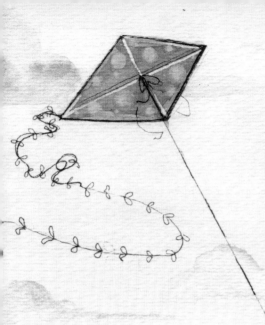

The umbrella is like a kite, doing tricks up in the air.
Isabella and Elvis held the string tight and ran without a care.

The umbrella changed into a weeping willow, providing shelter from the rain. Isabella and Elvis ate a picnic lunch, and laughed without refrain.

The umbrella transformed into a sail, and Elvis the first mate. They searched for sunken treasure, but must be home by eight.

The umbrella is like a helmet,
with Isabella atop her motorbike.
With Elvis in the sidecar, they
mosey down the turnpike.

The umbrella transformed into a polka dot cloud
that brings the shining sun.
Isabella and Elvis start to head home,
their adventures were almost done.

The umbrella became a princess wand,
and Elvis her trusty horse.
He took Isabella back to her castle, and
never went off course.

"It's time to come in!" mommy called, looking at the setting sun.
A tired, wet and happy young girl exclaimed, "We had lots of fun!"

After dinner, a bath,
and 5 favorite stories,
it is finally time for bed.

Pajamas are on and teeth are brushed, and many "goodnights" are said.

We love you so much, our busy little girl,
Mommy and Daddy whispered in her ear.

But Isabella and Elvis were sound asleep;
she was not awake to hear.

Author Carla Forrest lives in the San Francisco Bay Area with her family and 2 wonderful big brown dogs. She was inspired to write *Isabella and her Polka Dot Umbrella* by her own busy Isabella, who is her daily inspiration. When she is not spending time with her family, she works as an occupational therapist for a local school district, helping students with special needs.

CPSIA information can be obtained
at www.ICGtesting.com
Printed in the USA
398896LV00002B/4

9 781935 547327